David McPhail's
FAVORITE TALES

SCHOLASTIC INC.

New York Toronto London Auckland Sydney
Mexico City New Delhi Hong Kong Buenos Aires

The Tale of Peter Rabbit, ISBN-13: 978-0-590-41101-1, Illustrations copyright © 1986 by David McPhail. Art direction/design by Diana Hrisinko.
Little Red Riding Hood, ISBN-13: 978-0-590-48116-8, Copyright © 1995 by David McPhail.
Goldilocks and the Three Bears, ISBN-13: 978-0-590-48117-5, Copyright © 1995 by David McPhail.
The Three Little Pigs, ISBN-13: 978-0-590-48118-2, Copyright © 1995 by David McPhail.

12 11 10 9 8 7 6 5 4 3   9 10 11 12 13 14/0

Printed in Singapore   46

This edition created exclusively for Barnes & Noble, Inc.
2009 Barnes & Noble Books
ISBN-13: 978-0-7607-6124-3
This edition printing, August 2009

David McPhail's
FAVORITE TALES

The Tale
of Peter
Rabbit

Little Red
Riding Hood

Goldilocks
and the
Three Bears

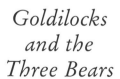

The Three
Little Pigs

THE TALE OF
PETER RABBIT

by Beatrix Potter

Illustrated by David McPhail

ONCE UPON A TIME there were four little
Rabbits, and their names were —
     Flopsy,
        Mopsy,
           Cottontail,
             and Peter.

They lived with their mother in a sandbank,
underneath the root of a very big fir tree.

"Now, my dears," said old Mrs. Rabbit one morning, "you may go into the fields or down the lane, but don't go into Mr. McGregor's garden: your father had an accident there; he was put in a pie by Mrs. McGregor."

"Now run along, and don't get into mischief.
I am going out."

9

Then old Mrs. Rabbit took a basket and her umbrella, and went through the wood to the baker's. She bought a loaf of brown bread and five currant buns.

Flopsy, Mopsy, and Cottontail, who were good
little bunnies, went down the lane to gather
blackberries.

But Peter, who was very naughty,
ran straight away to Mr. McGregor's garden,
and squeezed under the gate!

First he ate some lettuces and
some French beans; and
then he ate some radishes; and
then, feeling rather sick, he
went to look for some parsley.

But round the end of a cucumber frame, whom should he meet but Mr. McGregor!

Mr. McGregor was on his hands and knees planting out young cabbages, but he jumped up and ran after Peter, waving a rake and calling out, "Stop thief!"

Peter was most dreadfully frightened; he rushed all over the garden, for he had forgotten the way back to the gate.

He lost one of his shoes among the cabbages, and the other shoe amongst the potatoes.

After losing them, he ran on four legs and went faster, so that I think he might have got away altogether if he had not unfortunately run into a gooseberry net, and got caught by the large buttons on his jacket. It was a blue jacket with brass buttons, quite new.

Peter gave himself up for lost, and shed big tears; but his sobs were overheard by some friendly sparrows, who flew to him in great excitement, and implored him to exert himself.

Mr. McGregor came up with a sieve, which he intended to pop upon the top of Peter; but Peter wriggled out just in time, leaving his jacket behind him, and rushed into the toolshed, and jumped into a can.

It would have been a beautiful thing to hide in, if it had not had so much water in it.

Mr. McGregor was quite sure that Peter was somewhere in the toolshed, perhaps hidden underneath a flowerpot. He began to turn them over carefully, looking under each.

Presently Peter sneezed — "Kertyschoo!" Mr. McGregor was after him in no time, and tried to put his foot upon Peter, who jumped out of a window, upsetting three plants. The window was too small for Mr. McGregor, and he was tired of running after Peter. He went back to his work.

Peter sat down to rest. He was out of breath and trembling with fright, and he had not the least idea which way to go. Also, he was very damp with sitting in that can.

After a time he began to wander about, going lippity — lippity — not very fast, and looking all around.

He found a door in a wall; but it was locked, and there was no room for a fat little rabbit to squeeze underneath.

An old mouse was running in and out over the stone doorstep, carrying peas and beans to her family in the wood. Peter asked her the way to the gate, but she had such a large pea in her mouth that she could not answer. She only shook her head at him.

Peter began to cry.

Then he tried to find his way straight across the garden, but he became more and more puzzled. Presently, he came to a pond where Mr. McGregor filled his water cans. A white cat was staring at some goldfish; she sat very,

very still, but now and then the tip of her tail twitched as if it were alive. Peter thought it best to go away without speaking to her; he had heard about cats from his cousin, little Benjamin Bunny.

He went back towards the toolshed, but suddenly, quite close to him, he heard the noise of a hoe — scr-r-ritch, scratch, scratch, scritch. Peter scuttered underneath the bushes.

But presently, as nothing happened, he came out, and climbed upon a wheelbarrow, and peeped over. The first thing he saw was Mr. McGregor hoeing onions. His back was turned towards Peter, and beyond him was the gate!

Peter got down very quietly off the wheelbarrow, and started running as fast as he could go, along a straight walk behind some black-currant bushes.

Mr. McGregor caught sight of him at the corner, but Peter did not care. He slipped underneath the gate, and was safe at last in the wood outside the garden.

Mr. McGregor hung up the little jacket and the shoes for a scarecrow to frighten the blackbirds.

Peter never stopped running or looked behind him till he got home to the big fir tree.

He was so tired that he flopped down upon the nice soft sand on the floor of the rabbit hole, and shut his eyes. His mother was busy cooking; she wondered what he had done with his clothes. It was the second little jacket and pair of shoes that Peter had lost in a fortnight!

I am sorry to say that Peter was not very well during the evening.

His mother put him to bed, and made some camomile tea; and she gave a dose of it to Peter!

"One tablespoonful to be taken at bedtime."

But Flopsy, Mopsy, and Cottontail had bread and milk and blackberries for supper.

THE END.

LITTLE RED
RIDING HOOD

Retold and Illustrated by David McPhail

For Grace, who knows exactly
—D.M.

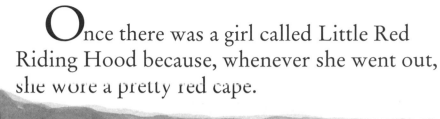

Once there was a girl called Little Red Riding Hood because, whenever she went out, she wore a pretty red cape.

One day her mother baked some cookies and asked Little Red Riding Hood to take them to Grandmother, who was ill and could not leave her bed.

"Stay on the path and don't dawdle,"
instructed Little Red Riding Hood's mother.
And the girl started off.

Little Red Riding Hood was about halfway to Grandmother's house when she met a wolf, but as she didn't know what a bad sort of animal he was, she did not feel afraid.

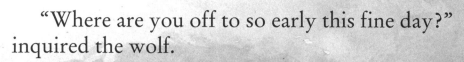

"Where are you off to so early this fine day?"
inquired the wolf.

"I'm taking some cookies to my grandmother," answered Little Red Riding Hood.

"And where does your grandmother live?" the wolf persisted.

"Her house stands beneath the three oak trees," said Little Red Riding Hood.

As she was innocently explaining all this, the wolf was thinking, *If I can get there before her, I'll eat the grandmother for my main course and this tender young morsel for my dessert.*

"Your grandmother would surely love a bouquet of flowers," the wolf said to Little Red Riding Hood.

And that set Little Red Riding Hood to thinking about it.

So Little Red Riding Hood ventured farther and farther off the path to pick flowers, while the wolf went hastily to Grandmother's house and knocked on the door.

"Who's there?" called the grandmother in a very weak voice.

"It's your dear granddaughter," lied the wolf.
"Please open the door."

"Come in," said the grandmother.
"The door is not locked."

As soon as the door opened, the grandmother realized her mistake.

For instead of her darling Little Red Riding Hood, a wicked wolf stepped into the room. And though the grandmother's body was weak, she ran into the wardrobe and locked the door.

The wolf would have torn the door right off its hinges, but through the window, he saw Little Red Riding Hood walking down the path.

So the wolf put on the grandmother's cap and glasses, which had fallen to the floor, climbed into the bed, and pulled the covers up to his chin.

When she got to her grandmother's house,
Little Red Riding Hood was surprised to see an
open door. Nevertheless, she stepped inside.

"Good morning, Grandmother," she called. But there was no answer. Little Red Riding Hood stepped closer to the bed.

As the curtain had been drawn around the bed, Little Red Riding Hood could not see clearly in the dim light. "Oh, Grandmother," she exclaimed, "what big *ears* you have!"

"All the better to *hear* you with," said the wolf.

"Oh, Grandmother," said Little Red Riding Hood, "what big *eyes* you have!"

"All the better to *see* you with," said the wolf.

"Oh, Grandmother," said Little Red Riding Hood, "what big *teeth* you have!"

"All the better to *eat* you with!" said the wolf and he threw back the covers.

But Little Red Riding Hood was too quick for the wolf, and before he could catch her, she crawled under the bed.

The angry wolf went after her, but as he was much bigger than Little Red Riding Hood, he got stuck.

Little Red Riding Hood came out from under the bed and jumped on top of it. She jumped up and down, and shouted at the top of her voice, "Help! Help! There's a big bad wolf in here, and I fear he has eaten my grandmother!"

Little Red Riding Hood's grandmother, on hearing this, came out of the wardrobe.

Meanwhile, everyone who happened to be in the forest that day, including a woodcutter with a mighty sharp ax, heard Little Red Riding Hood's cries and ran to help.

They had nearly reached the cottage when the wolf finally managed to squeeze out from under the bed and stagger through the door.

The last time Little Red Riding Hood saw
the wolf, he was running down the path,
followed closely by a hostile crowd.

And Little Red Riding Hood never saw
or heard from him again.

GOLDILOCKS AND THE THREE BEARS

Retold and Illustrated by David McPhail

For Edie, who makes it all work
—D.M.

Once upon a time, three bears lived in a cozy house in the middle of the forest. They were a great big father bear, a medium-sized mother bear, and a little baby bear.

Every morning the three bears ate porridge for breakfast.

The father bear ate his porridge from a large blue bowl, the mother bear ate her porridge from a medium-sized red bowl, and the baby bear ate his porridge from a little silver bowl.

One morning the three bears decided to go for a walk while their porridge cooled.

The father bear put on his great big hat ... the mother bear put on her medium-sized bonnet ... and the baby bear flipped his little cap onto his little head. Then they all went down the path that ran past their cozy house.

Also on the path that day, but coming from the other direction, was a little girl. She was called Goldilocks because she had golden hair that hung down past her shoulders.

You might say that Goldilocks was a spoiled child because she always got her way. Her mother and father were good people, but they couldn't bear to say *no* to her. So Goldilocks grew up thinking she could have whatever she wanted.

On this particular day, Goldilocks had been walking through the forest when she came upon the house of the three bears.

"I wonder who lives here," she said to herself. "And I wonder if they will give me something to eat."

So Goldilocks walked boldly up the front step.

The bears—who trusted everyone and were very trustworthy themselves—never locked their door, and on this day, had not even bothered to latch it.

Therefore, when Goldilocks knocked, the door swung open.

"Hello," she called. "Anybody home?"

As there was no answer, Goldilocks stepped inside and looked around.

To her delight, she saw three bowls of porridge on the kitchen table.

Goldilocks tasted the porridge in the big bowl. "Ouch!" she cried. "Too HOT!"

She tasted the porridge in the medium-sized bowl. "Uggh!" she groaned. "Too COLD!"

Then Goldilocks tasted the porridge in the little bowl. "Ummmm," she cooed. "Just right!"

And she ate it all up.

Then, because she had walked so far, Goldilocks decided to sit down to rest her tired feet.

First she climbed up into the great big chair of the great big father bear. But the springs were so stiff, she felt as if she were sitting on a pile of bricks.

"Too hard," she said, as she moved to the middle-sized chair.

But she sank so deep into its cushions that she nearly disappeared.

"Too soft!" she squealed.

Then Goldilocks went over to the wee little chair and plunked herself down.

"Perfect!" she sighed.

But she had sat down too hard, for a moment later the bottom fell right out of the chair and sent the startled Goldilocks crashing to the floor.

"Dumb chair," she grumbled, as she picked herself up and started up the stairs.

In the room at the top of the stairs were three beds. Being tired still, Goldilocks was determined to get some rest.

She climbed onto the biggest bed, but it was like lying on boards. "Much too hard," she said.

The middle-sized bed was so soft she feared she might smother.

"Too soft," she said, gasping for air. Then Goldilocks tried the little bed. It was so comfortable that she soon fell asleep.

At about this time, the three bears returned home to eat their porridge. The father bear noticed that his spoon had been left standing in his bowl.

"Someone's been tasting my porridge!" he thundered, in his great big voice.

"Someone's been tasting my porridge, too!" the mother bear said in her middle-sized voice.

"Someone's been tasting my porridge," the baby bear cried in his wee little voice, "and has eaten it all up!"

Realizing that someone had come into their house while they were out, the three bears began to look around.

The father bear noticed that the hard cushion in the big chair was not as he had left it. "Someone's been sitting in my chair!" he growled.

The book that the mother bear had placed on the arm of her chair was on the floor. "Someone's been sitting in my chair, too," she said.

Then the baby bear looked at his chair. "Someone's been sitting in my chair," he cried, "and has sat the bottom right out of it!"

The three bears decided to go upstairs to see if anything else had been disturbed.

The pillow on the biggest bed was not in its proper place. "Someone's been sleeping in my bed!" the father bear grumbled.

And the bedspread on the middle-sized bed was not as neat and tidy as mother bear had left it.

"Someone's been sleeping in my bed, too!" said the mother bear.

Then the little bear looked in his bed.

"Someone's been sleeping in my bed," he cried, "and here she is!"

At that instant, Goldilocks opened her eyes.
When she saw the three bears staring down at
her, she scrambled out of the bed and ran down
the stairs, and she didn't stop running till she
was all the way home.

Despite their experience with Goldilocks, the three bears went on as before, and to this day, they still don't lock their door.

As for Goldilocks, she learned a lesson she never forgot, and she never again entered anyone's house without first being invited.

THE THREE
LITTLE PIGS

Retold and Illustrated by David McPhail

For Kiko, Nigel, and Amos:
Three of a kind, all different
—D.M.

Once there were three little pigs who lived
at home with their mother. When the little pigs
were all grown up, they decided to strike out
on their own.

One morning at sunrise, they said good-bye
to their mother and walked away, arm in arm.

When they came to a crossroads, the three
little pigs took different paths, promising to
visit each other very soon.

The first little pig saw a man cutting straw in a field. The little pig offered to help if the man would give him straw to build his house. And the man agreed.

The little pig carried the straw to a shady
riverbank where he quickly built a little straw
house and settled in.

The second little pig came upon a woman collecting sticks along the edge of a deep, dark forest. The little pig offered to help the woman if she would give him sticks to build his house.

The woman agreed, and by-and-by, she gave the second little pig some bundles of sticks. The little pig quickly threw the sticks together in the shape of a house, crawled in, and went to sleep.

The third little pig met a man who was building a tall chimney out of bricks. But the man was afraid to climb the ladder.

"If you will give me enough bricks to build a small house, I will climb the ladder for you," said the third little pig. And the man agreed.

The man gave the third little pig stacks and stacks of bricks that the little pig took to the top of the highest hill. *This is a good place for my house*, thought the third little pig. And she began to build.

The next morning, the first little pig was awakened by a noise outside his house.

He peeked out between pieces of straw, and when he saw the wolf, the little pig trembled, for he knew that wolves were no friends of pigs.

"Little pig, little pig, let me come in," said the wolf.

"Not by the hair of my chinny chin chin," answered the first little pig.

"Then I'll huff, and I'll puff, and I'll blow your house in!" roared the wolf.

So he huffed and he puffed. And while the wolf was blowing the house down, the first little pig ran away and dove into the stream.

When it was safe, the first little pig cautiously made his way to his brother's house of sticks and told his brother how the wolf blew his house down.

At that instant, they heard a noise.
"It's the wolf!" whispered the first little pig.
"There's nobody home," called the second little pig. "Go away!"

But the wolf didn't budge. "Little pig, little pig, let me come in!" he snarled.

"Not by the hair of my chinny chin chin," replied the second little pig.

"Then I'll huff, and I'll puff, and I'll blow your house in!" roared the wolf.

So he huffed, and he puffed, and as with the straw house, he blew the stick house right down to the ground. The two little pigs ran in opposite directions, which so confused the wolf that, by the time he decided which one to chase, they had both disappeared into the woods.

Later that day, the first little pig and the second little pig arrived at the house of the third little pig. The third little pig welcomed her brothers into her sturdy brick house.

While they told her the story of the wolf,
she lit a fire in the fireplace and set a big kettle
of water on to boil.

Then the three little pigs started to cut some vegetables to make a stew. Suddenly there was a pounding at the door. It was the wolf! The first little pig and the second little pig were terrified.

But the third little pig felt safe in her house of bricks. "Go away, Wolf," she said. "Don't bother us!"

By this time, the wolf was very hungry and very angry that the other little pigs had gotten away from him.

"Little pig, little pig, let me come in!" he roared at the top of his voice.

"Not by the hair of my chinny chin chin," answered the third little pig calmly.

"Then I'll huff, and I'll puff, and I'll blow your house in!" said the wolf.

But no matter how hard he huffed—and no matter how hard he puffed—he couldn't blow the house down. The brick house was too strong. The exhausted wolf sat on the front step to rest.

When he had recovered somewhat from
all that huffing and puffing, the wolf walked
around the little brick house, looking for
another way in.

The windows were too small for him to squeeze through, but when the wolf looked up, he saw a big chimney sticking out of the roof. It was big enough for a big wolf like himself.

The three little pigs could hear footsteps above them. "Run!" cried the first little pig. "The wolf's coming down the chimney!"

"Hide!" squealed the second little pig. "If he catches us, he'll eat us all!"

But the third little pig was not afraid.

"Finish cutting those vegetables," she said, "while I put some more wood on the fire."

The water in the kettle was boiling
furiously when the clever wolf came
sliding down the chimney—SPLASH!—
right into the big pot.

The third little pig slammed the lid on.
And that was the end of the wicked wolf.